The Journey Home

Alison Lester

Houghton Mifflin Company

Boston

Library of Congress Cataloging-in-Publication Data

Lester, Alison.
    The journey home / Alison Lester. — 1st American ed.
    p.   cm.
    "Originally published in Australia in 1990 by Oxford University Press"
— Tp. verso.
    Summary: After falling through a pit and landing at the North
Pole, Wild and Woolly have a long but interesting journey back home,
punctuated by overnight stays with a number of colorful individuals.
    HC ISBN 0-395-53355-4   PA ISBN 0-395-74517-9
    [1. Voyages and travel — Fiction.]   I. Title.
PZ7.L56284Jo   1990   89-28355
[E] — dc20   CIP
                                                          AC

Printed in Singapore
TWP 10 9 8 7 6 5 4 3 2 1

The author wishes to thank Rita Scharf of Oxford University Press
for her assistance with this book.

For Rachel & Daniel

One day Wild and Woolly dug such a big hole in their sandpit, that when they fell into it, they came out at the North Pole.

Immediately they set out on
the journey home,

across the cold and slippery ice,

past the growling polar bears.

They came that night to a cheerful house.
Reindeer stamped in the chilly air.

"Season's greetings," boomed Father Christmas. "Come inside and stay."

Wild and Woolly ate roast turkey and plum pudding for dinner. They played with next year's toys until they fell asleep.

Then on again went
Wild and Woolly, across
the snowy countryside,

into a green and gloomy forest,

following a twisting path.

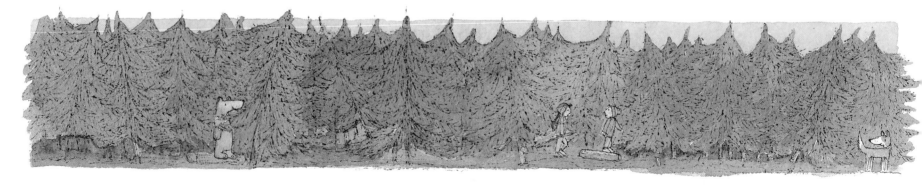

They came that night
to an ancient tree.
Fairy lights hung in its
branches, and silver
bells tinkled in the
evening breeze.

"Well, bless my wings and will-o'-wisps," laughed the Good Fairy. "Come inside and stay."

Wild and Woolly had angel cakes and sugar kisses for supper. They slept in beds as soft as clouds.

Then on again went
Wild and Woolly,
leaving the forest far
behind,

over a bridge and down a
hillside,

on to an open valley road.

They came that night
to a royal castle.
Its drawbridge hung
over a rushing stream.

"Ah, Lord Wild and Lady Woolly!" cried Prince Charming.
"Come inside and stay."

Wild and Woolly feasted on royal trifle
and rhubarb fool, and climbed upstairs
to bed.

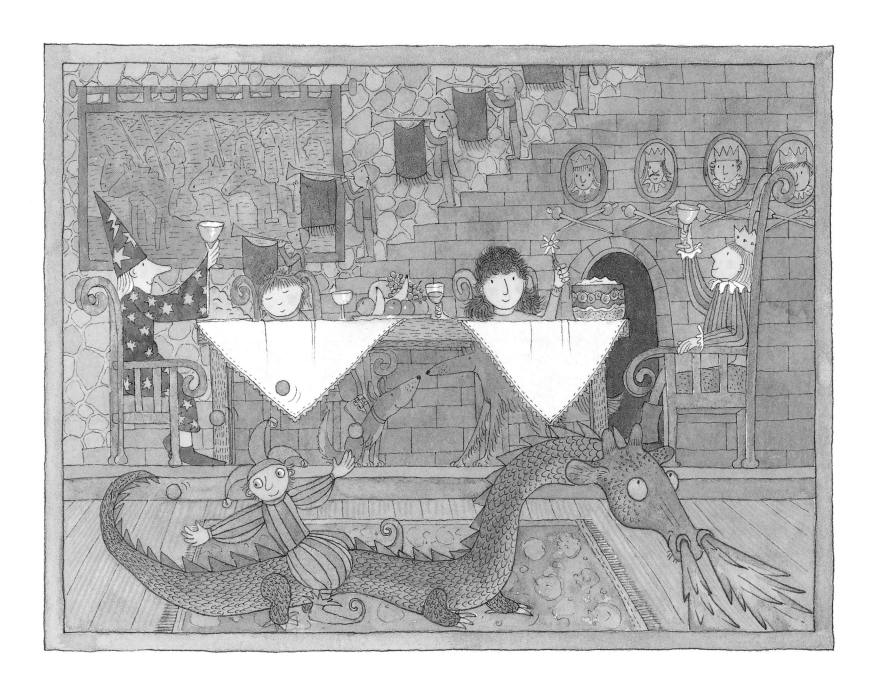

Then on again went
Wild and Woolly, over
the wet and soggy
marsh,

tumbling down the shifting
sand dunes,

and on to the windy beach.

They came that night to a weather-beaten rock.
Singing and splashing noises came from inside the cave.

"Better than a fish or a wish," sang the Little Mermaid. "Come inside and stay."

Wild and Woolly shared sea grapes served on mother-of-pearl dishes. The sound of the waves soothed them to sleep.

Then on again went Wild and Woolly, splashing through the shallow pools,

over a rough and rocky headland,

and round to a sheltered bay.

They came that night to a creaking ship.
A tattered flag flew from the mast.

"Yo ho, me hearties," called the Pirate King. "Come inside and stay."

Wild and Woolly had salami sausage and pickled cucumbers for dinner. Their hammocks rocked them to sleep as the ship crossed the ocean.

Then on again went Wild and Woolly, up a hill and away from the sea,

following some crooked wheel marks,

into a forest of rustling trees.

They came that night to a horse and caravan. Smoke curled from the crooked chimney, and a crystal ball glowed in the window.

"I *knew* you were coming," said the Gypsy Queen. "Come inside and stay."

Wild and Woolly ate goulash and dumplings for supper. They slept in bunks under patchwork eiderdowns.

Then on again went Wild and Woolly,
running over the
rolling hills,

through the paddocks and under
fences,

hurrying on to home.

They came that night to a house they knew.
A welcoming light shone through the open door.

"You're home at last!" cried their parents. "Come inside and stay."

Wild and Woolly had mugs of hot chocolate before climbing into their very own beds.

It was good to be home.